Louie's BIG day!

by Maria I. Morgan   Illustrated by Sherrie Molitor

FREE
audiobook
@
www.mariaimorgan.wix.com/louie-the-lawnmower

© 2014 by Maria I. Morgan. All rights reserved. No portion of this book may be reproduced, stored in a retrieval system, or transmitted in any form or by any means - electronic, mechanical, photocopy, recording, scanning, or other - except for brief quotations in critical reviews or articles, without the prior written permission of the author.

© 2014 Illustrations by Sherrie Molitor. All rights reserved.

Today was his big day!

Louie the Lawnmower was a little anxious. He hadn't slept a wink last night. Over and over he practiced rolling in a straight line, until he bumped into the garage door with a bang.

His people called it mowing, but Louie had heard it was like eating. His stomach got a little queasy as he thought about eating for the first time...

Would he like grass? What would it taste like? Would the smell of grass make him sneeze?

Louie had just come to his new home from the hardware store yesterday.

It had been hard leaving all of his friends in the lawn care section: Eddie Edger, Bobbie Blower, Terri Trowel, and his best friend, Ruthie Rake.

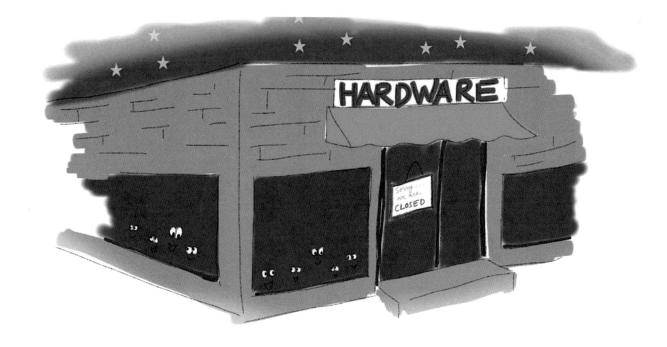

He closed his eyes and smiled, remembering all the pranks he and his pals had played when the lights went out at the end of the day...

There was the time Bobbie Blower was feeling mischievous and blew all the gardening gloves off their display stand.

They had spent the rest of the night helping all 100 pairs of gloves back onto their hooks!

How could he forget the night Eddie Edger and Ruthie Rake snuck off to the next aisle and made scary scratching noises that made him and the others scream with fright?

Today was different. Louie the Lawnmower was by himself. He missed his friends, but he had a job to do.

The door opened and out walked his people. The man was ready to mow. The lady was going to the store.

Louie liked the way the gas felt as it sloshed down into his tank. It made him feel full of energy!

Once he was pushed out into the grass, Louie forgot all about being nervous. He glided across the grass in straight lines – munching all the way.

Grass was great! It tasted amazingly good! He didn't sneeze a single time while mowing the entire lawn!

"This is what I've been made to do!" thought Louie, as the man pushed him back into the garage. Mowing grass was fun! "If only I could tell my friends about my adventure..." sighed Louie.

Just then, the lady returned from the store. She pulled into the garage and opened the trunk.

What she pulled out of the trunk made
Louie sputter with delight!

His friends smiled back at him: Eddie Edger, Bobbie Blower, Terri Trowel, Henri Hose, two pairs of the gardening gloves, and his best friend, Ruthie Rake.

"**N**ow we can finish the yard," said the lady. That afternoon, as Louie the Lawnmower rested and waited patiently for all of his friends to return to the garage, he couldn't help but smile.

Louie was happier than ever. He loved to munch grass, and he couldn't wait to make new memories with his friends!

Louie's Lesson Corner:

1. When I came home from the hardware store I was nervous about mowing grass. What was I worried about?

2. I thought about my days at the hardware store. Who did I miss?

3. After I cut the lawn, I realized I was made to mow grass. You're special just like me. What are some things God created you to do?

4. When I was done mowing, what surprise made me sputter with delight?

5. Friends are wonderful gifts from God. Name some of your friends and thank God for them!

See you soon,

Louie the Lawnmower

Psst...It's me, Louie! Have you heard the news? I'm online! I'd love to meet you.

Here's my address:

www.mariaimorgan.wix.com/louie-the-lawnmower

*Just share your email address with me, and I'll send you a link to my FREE audiobook!

About the Author

Maria I. Morgan was born with an active imagination that shows up in her endearing stories for children. Originally an inspirational author and speaker for adults, Maria has widened her circle to include kids. She lives in the muggy South with her husband, two retrievers, and two Maine coon kitties ~ the perfect mix to fuel her creativity for years to come!
www.mariaimorgan.wix.com/louie-the-lawnmower

About the Illustrator

Sherrie Molitor has been a member of both the Mid-Michigan Art Guild and the Society of Children's Book Writers and Illustrators. Her paintings have been displayed in numerous local Michigan galleries and venues. Her book illustrations generally involve self-publishing authors who have wonderful stories to tell. She works in a comfy home studio and is inspired by her surroundings.

www.sherriemolitor.wix.com/sherriemolitorart#!childrens-book-samples/c8ir

Made in the USA
Coppell, TX
21 August 2023

20601388R00019